The First Christmas

First published in Great Britain in 2002 by Brimax™,
A division of Autumn Publishing Limited
Appledram Barns, Chichester PO20 7EQ

Mc Graw Hill **Children's Publishing**

This edition published in the United States of America in 2003 by
Gingham Dog Press
an imprint of McGraw-Hill Children's Publishing,
a Division of The McGraw-Hill Companies
8787 Orion Place
Columbus, Ohio 43240-4027

www.MHkids.com

Library of Congress Cataloging-in-Publication Data is on file with the publisher.

Printed in China.

ISBN 0-7696-3128-2

1 2 3 4 5 6 7 8 9 10 BRI 09 08 07 06 05 04 03

The *McGraw·Hill* Companies

The First Christmas

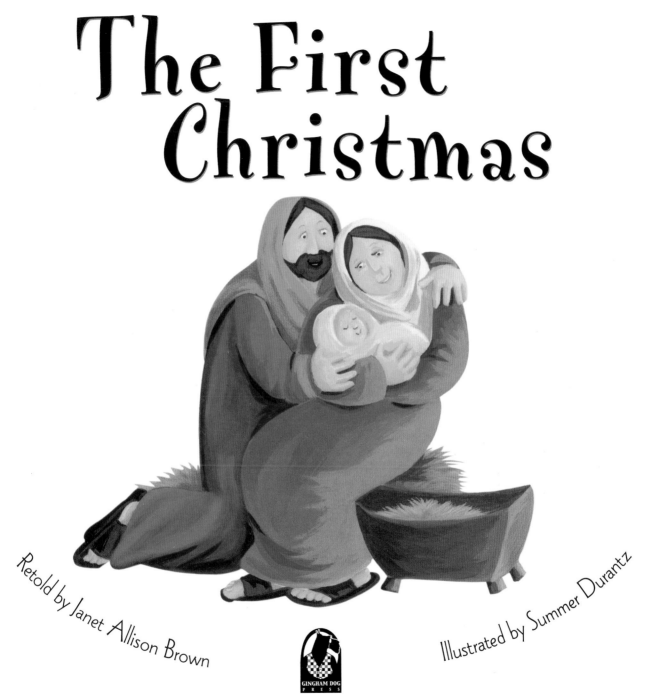

Retold by Janet Allison Brown

Illustrated by Summer Durantz

GINGHAM DOG PRESS

Columbus, Ohio

Christmas is a very special time of year, full of celebrations. People decorate trees, give presents, and sing Christmas carols. But do you know why we really celebrate Christmas?

The story began more than two thousand years ago in a town called Nazareth.

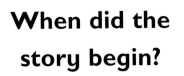

Mary, a kind young woman, was busy making plans for her wedding to a carpenter named Joseph. Suddenly, a golden angel appeared before her.

"I am the angel, Gabriel, and I have come to bring you a message," he said. "God has chosen you to be the mother of His Son, Jesus. This baby will be a great man one day!"

In which town did Mary, Jesus' mother, live?

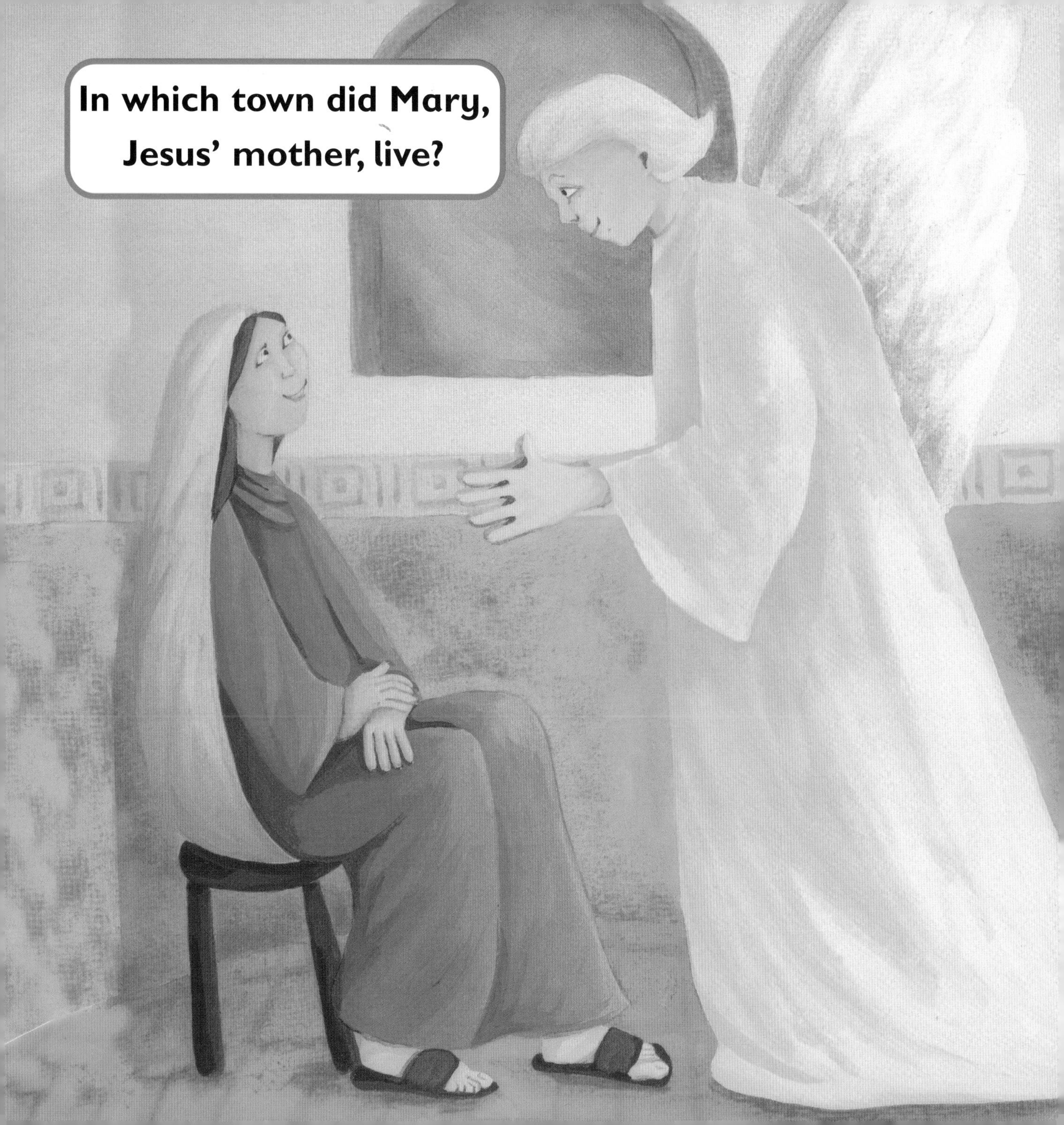

Mary was honored that God had chosen her for such an important task. Joseph was proud that God had chosen her, too. Shortly after they were married, the baby began to grow inside Mary.

One day, Joseph came home with some important news. "We must hurry to Bethlehem," he said. "The king wants to take a count of all his subjects."

The very next day the couple traveled to Bethlehem.

Where did Mary and Joseph travel to be counted?

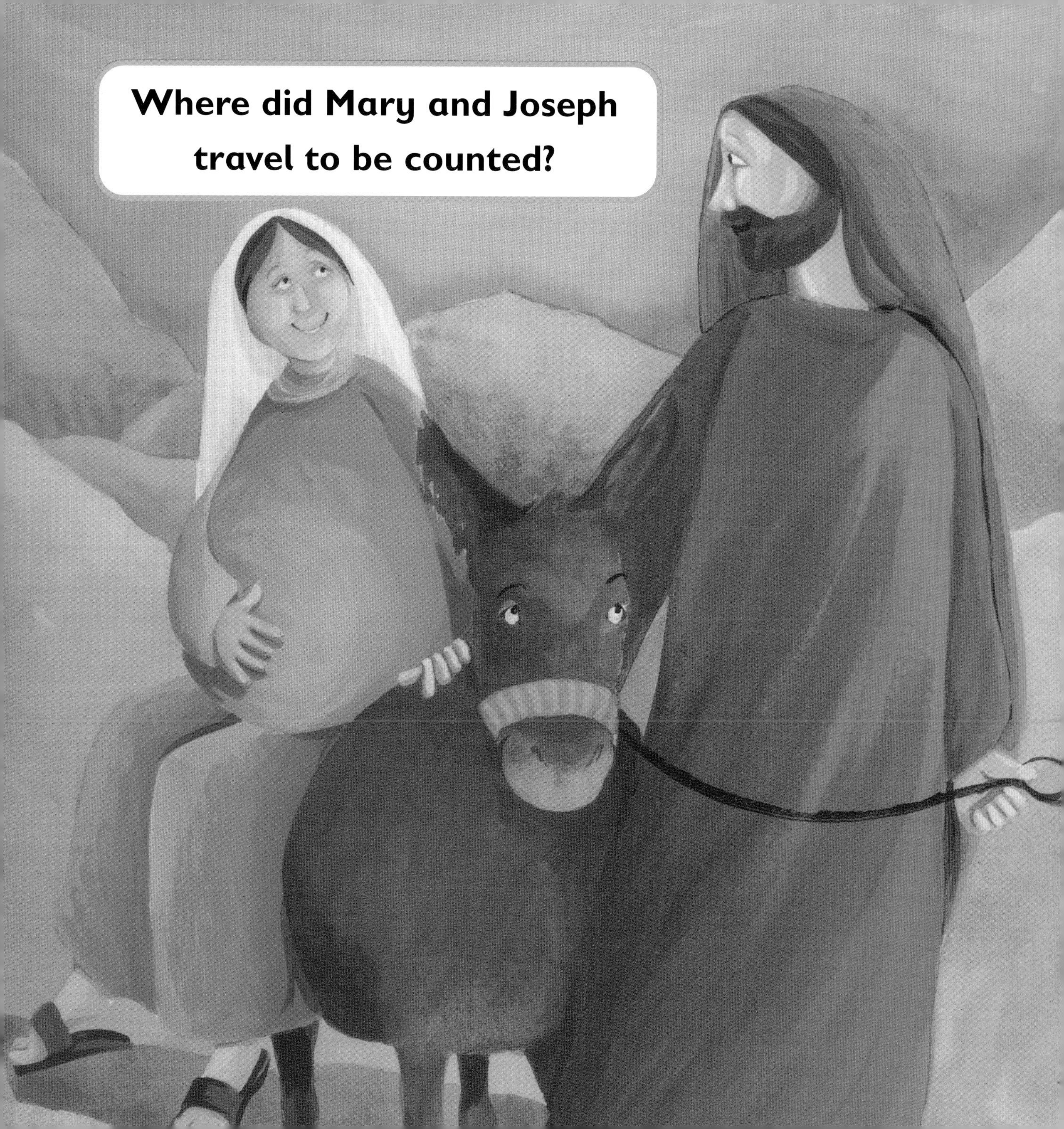

Everyone had come to Bethlehem to be counted, and the streets were crowded. Mary and Joseph searched for a place to stay, but all the inns were full.

"My wife is going to have a baby," Joseph told an innkeeper. "Please, do you have somewhere for us to stay?"

The innkeeper thought for a while. "There is room in the stable with my animals," he said. "They are very gentle, and there's plenty of fresh hay to make a comfortable bed."

Where did Mary and Joseph sleep for the night?

So, Joseph made Mary a bed in the hay, and late that night, Jesus was born. Mary and Joseph kissed their baby and wrapped him in warm blankets.

Then, they made a bed for him in the manger, surrounded by the animals.

Little did the innkeeper know, the baby that was sleeping in his stable was God's Son, who had come to bring peace to the world!

Where did Jesus sleep in the stable?

In the hills surrounding Bethlehem, shepherds stood watching their flocks of sheep. Suddenly, a big, bright star appeared in the sky.

Then, the air was filled with singing angels, telling the shepherds to follow the star.

The shepherds followed the star to the little stable. There they knelt in wonder before the manger.

What did the shepherds follow to reach the stable?

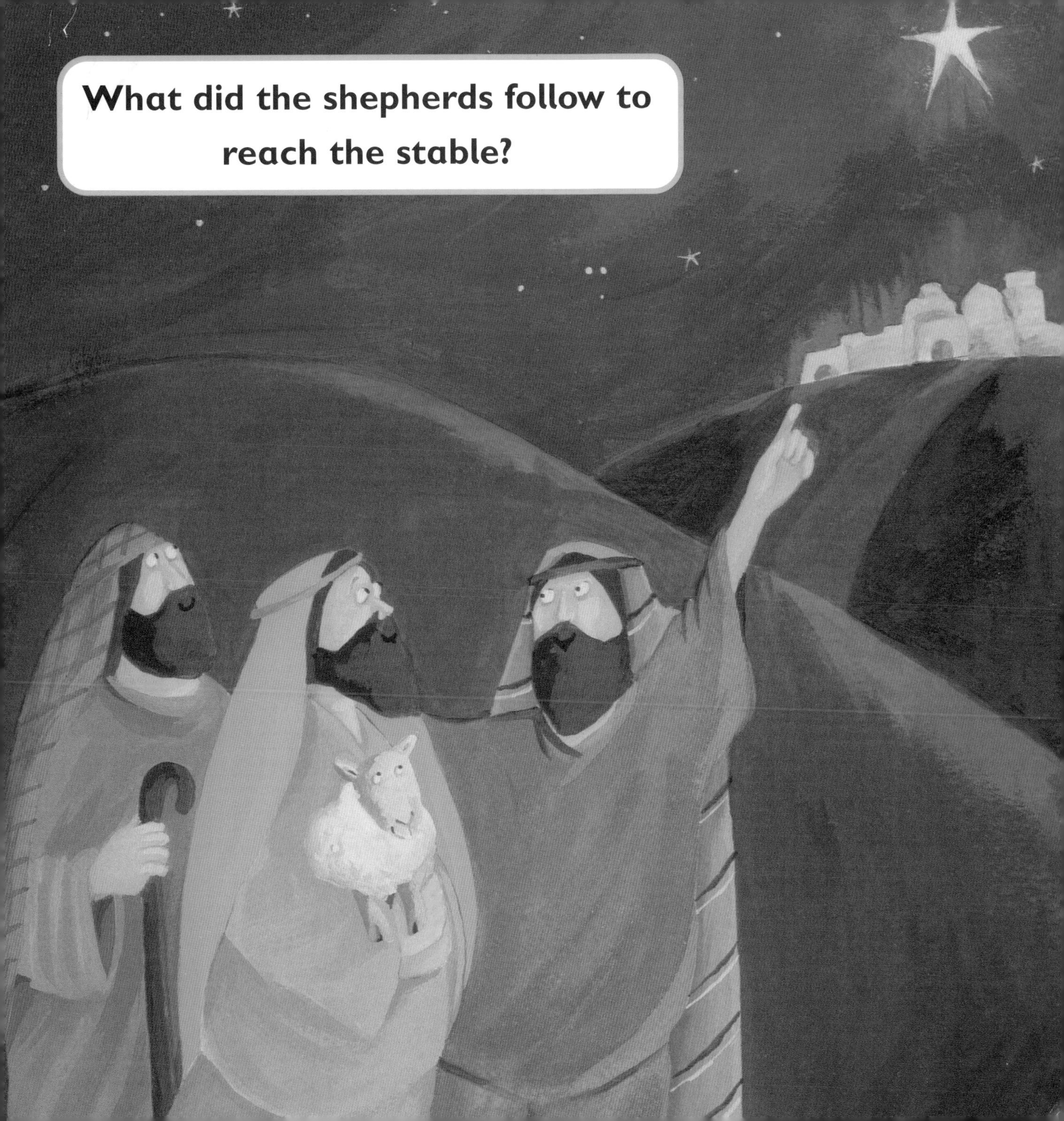

Three wise men from distant lands were also following the star. They rode their camels across deserts and hills to reach the stable in Bethlehem.

When they arrived, they knelt down before Jesus. "We bring you gifts of gold, frankincense, and myrrh," they told him.

Then, the wise men thanked God for this special child, who would one day be the King of Heaven.

How many gifts did
the wise men bring?

The tiny baby born in a stable grew up to be a great leader, who worked many miracles. He showed people how to love, take care of each other, and live peaceful lives.

This Christmas, as you open your presents, remember that you are really celebrating the birth of a very special baby, who is God's gift to you and me.

Glossary

angel   A spiritual messenger of God.

Bethlehem   The city in Israel where Jesus was born.

Christmas   The Christian holiday that celebrates Jesus' birth.

frankincense   Fragrant gum from a tree used to make perfume.

Gabriel   The angel that tells Mary about God's plan for her.

gold   A precious and valuable metal.

inn   A place where people who are traveling can stay.

innkeeper   The owner of a place where people who are traveling can stay.

Jesus — God's Son, born to Mary and Joseph.

Joseph — Husband to Mary.

manger — A feeding box used to hold food for animals.

Mary — Mother of Jesus; wife to Joseph.

myrrh — Fragrant gum from a tree used to make perfume.

Nazareth — A town in Israel where Jesus lived as a child.

shepherd — A person who takes care of sheep.

stable — A building where animals are kept and fed.

wise men — Very important people who visited baby Jesus in Bethlehem.